To the Moon and Back

By: Jennifer Stables

Jenny Dale Designs

www.JennyDaleDesigns.com

ISBN: 978-0-9958047-4-6

This Book Belongs To:

_____

You Are Loved.

The day is done
And as the sun
Sinks slowly in the west,
Their hearts speak of
These words of love
As they lie down to rest...

"Even when I stomp and cry?

Even when I shout?"

My love for you is endless.
This, you must always know;

And carry with you all your life,
Wherever you may go.

If I took all my love for you
And held it in my hands;
My dear, how it would overflow...

And soon flood all the land!

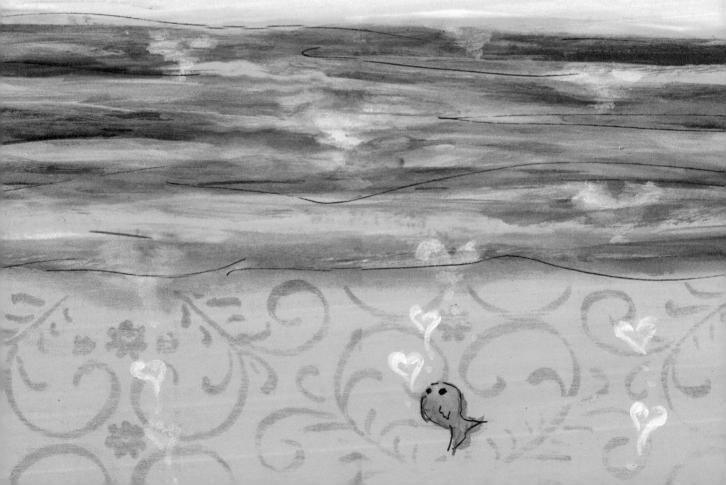

It wouldn't even fit
Inside a pond or lake or sea.

Even air could never hold
The love for you, from me.

My child, if you know one thing
And only to be true,
To the moon and back, sweetheart...

That's how much
I love you.

I Love you to the Moon and Back...

When I began my business, Jenny Dale Designs, my first son was only 5 months old. I wanted to tell a story with every illustration I created, so I decided to write a poem to accompany each one. One image was of a steam-punk style outer space scene. A planet in the corner of the drawing had a small flag sticking out from it. The flag read, "I love you to the moon and back".

I contemplated how I would write a poem to accompany this drawing for days. Then one night as I was putting my son to bed I began to wonder if he'd ever truly know how much I loved him. Would he ever know that he changed my world? Could I ever put to words how his presence opened a floodgate of emotions in my heart? To simply say 'I love you to the moon and back' was not enough. He needed to know that my love for him was too big to hold in my hands, too abundant for the depths of the oceans, and too vast for the confines of our atmosphere.

And so, my poem, 'To the Moon and Back' was born, and it has since been shared with thousands of people worldwide. We were blessed with a second son two years later and, again, the love was overwhelming.

This book was written for my sons, James and Myles, but really it is for every parent and every child.

You are SO loved.

JENNIFER DALE STABLES-B.F.A, B.ED.

Jennifer Dale Stables is an author, artist, and educator living in Okotoks, Alberta, Canada. A former classroom teacher, Jennifer has dedicated her artistic endeavors to creating artwork and illustrations for children, and working in schools as an artist in residence. Through her business, Jenny Dale Designs, she creates whimsical artwork and writes poetry to accompany each one of her lovable creations.

www.JennyDaleDesigns.com

MORE BOOKS BY JENNIFER STABLES:

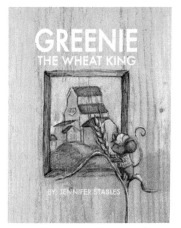  

shop.JennyDaleDesigns.com

CPSIA information can be obtained
at www.ICGtesting.com
Printed in the USA
LVHW070717281018
595107LV00002B/2/P